MY RISING STAR

Beauty faces a very bleak future. Born to poor parents and raised in a house where two square meals a day was considered an unaffordable luxury, Beauty must give up her hopes of becoming a medical doctor and get married to a man whom she had never met and was twice her age in order for her to help sustain the family. Worst of all, the man was an illegal immigrant struggling to find his feet in America. Left with no choice and armed with a burning desire to get her family out of poverty, Beauty eventually leaves for the United States.

Things, however, were not as rosy as Beauty had anticipated. Her fiancée wasn't ready to take responsibility for her yet and things got worse when she gets pregnant six months to their wedding. Her fiancée is devastated and wants to abort the pregnancy. But Beauty is determined to keep the child even if it means becoming a single mother. Despite the bleak hope, she was determined to try all she could to make the future brighter. But a prophet had already fore saw a prophecy.

How the Story Unfolded:

- Beauty's early life
- How Beauty lost her father and dropped out of school
- Wemi asks for Beauty's had in marriage on behalf of her son Felix, who was based in America
- Beauty agrees to marry Felix
- Beauty's visits a Prophet for prayers and advice over her impending marriage
- The prophet makes sexual advances towards her
- Beauty decides to go ahead with the marriage against the Prophet's words
- Felix is unable to attend his own engagement due to paper works problems
- After two unsuccessful attempts, Beauty was eventually granted visa and she go to America to be with her fiancé
- Felix was shocked that his fiancée was much younger than her anticipated
- Beauty realizes that Felix doesn't love him
- She makes friend with a Nigerian lady in her neighborhood
- She becomes pregnant and Felix tries to abort the baby without her knowledge
- Felix's mother, Wemi advises his son to take responsibility for his wife and child.
- Felix obeys his mother and sends Beauty to high school after she put to bed
- Beauty was granted scholarship and permanent residency
- Felix was granted permanent residency by virtue of Beauty being a permanent resident
- Beauty eventually achieves her childhood dreams of becoming a medical doctor.

CHAPTER ONE

BEAUTY kicked an empty polyethylene terephthalate bottle along the dusty road absentmindedly. A large round tray balanced on her head as she thronged along. Her worn out slippers and legs were covered in the unforgiving harmattan dust. The tray on her head contained her wares of smoked fish which had she always hawked for her mother every evening since she dropped out of secondary school three years ago. The proceeds she made from the sales was what her mother used in providing for her and her three younger siblings.

Benjamin Beauty was the first child of her parents. Her father had died two days to her thirteenth birthday when he was crushed on his bicycle by a truck whose break was alleged to have failed. This made an already difficult life even more difficult for her and her siblings. Nicknamed BB by her peers while she was still in school, a brilliant and cheerful girl and was loved by all her teachers and classmates. Not only was she a brilliant girl but also a beautiful girl as well. Men consistently cast glances of admiration on her. Now at the tender age of seventeen, Beauty was even more a representation now than ever. She was indeed an epitome of beauty. Despite years of hawking in unfriendly weather conditions, Beauty's fair skin managed to retain Its radiance. Her black long hair was the envy of so many girls in the town and her blue eyes perfectly matched her round face. She had the stature of a model and her breasts were perky and succulent. No one could deny her beauty.

Everyone in the town talked about how even more beautiful she would have been if she were born to rich parents. Boys and young men and even married men threw their cards to win over the young lady. But Beauty was as determined as she was beautiful. Although she came from a very poor background, she was without an iota of doubt, a well brought up girl. Her dream was to become a medical doctor-a dream that was birthed when a flu broke out in their town seven years ago. So many people we're infected with it and the local chemists and nurses were unable to treat it despite the administration of various types of drugs they confidently said would tackle the disease. Local herbs also failed to combat the disease. After five people in the town were reported to have died in two days as a result of the flu, the whole town was thrown into a state of frenzy and despair. People stayed indoors most of the time. The religious ones held vigils of prayers, asking God to forgive them their sins and wipe away the incurable disease from their town.

The superstitious people said that the gods of the land were angry because of the atrocities that had been committed by the people in the town. And hence, they were being punished by the incurable disease and death. The chief priest said they needed to offer sacrifice to the gods to appease them. He then asked the whole town to contribute money to buy the things necessary for the sacrifice. A week after the purported sacrifice had been offered to appease the gods, four people were reported dead. It appeared like there was no end or cure in sight for this disease.

An end and cure will however come to the disease that had taken many lives in their town when the local chemists reported the case at the city's Health Center which was about thirty-five kilometers away from their town. Swiftly, the ministry of health reacted upon hearing about the case. Doctors, nurses and other health workers were quickly mobilized and sent to the town. They arrived with relief materials and a lot of drugs. People who had the disease were separated from the rest of the lot and quarantined. They were treated in their quarantine. People with severe cases had to be taken to the city for elaborate medical attention.

Beauty's mother had been struck down by the flu as well. With all local herbs and drugs failing to cure her, Beauty and her sibling cried all day, hoping their mother would not die like the other people who have been reported dead. Her father tried all he could. He went from one bush to another seeking herbs that might help her recover, but all were to no avail. Hope was however, restored to them as the health workers from the city arrived just in time to save the day. Her mother was among those that were quarantined for treatment. Within a week of the health workers' arrival, most of those infected with the disease had made full recoveries. Beauty's mother, Queen, was one of them. The family was so elated. Relieve flooded the whole town and the frenzy atmosphere was gradually replaced by a serene one.

Beauty was running an errand for her mother that hot afternoon when she met a lady dressed in white and wearing a nose mask. She had a cap made of what Beauty suspected was nylon on her head, but she was sure not if it was actually made of nylon. But it wasn't a refit cap. It was the kind of cap the health works from the city wore. She knew she had to be one of the health workers. The gods who have saved her mother from dying.
'Who are you?' The young Beauty asked innocently.
The woman turned around to see a young beautiful child of about ten or eleven standing beside her. The woman was a tall, her complexion was chocolate and Beauty could tell she smelled like drugs. She squatted beside her and took off her nose mask to reveal a warming smile. 'I'm Sharon.'
Beauty creased her forehead. That wasn't in any way close to the answer she was expecting. 'People say every one of you that came to treat us are gods, is it true?'
Sharon read the confusion on the face of the little girl and gave her another smile. 'It's not true. We are health workers, not gods.'
Her answer did nothing to clarify her confusions. 'Who are health workers?' Her little inquisitive voice rang out.
Sharon saw a tree stump nearby and held her hand as she led her to the stump. 'Come here, sit.' She helped her up and sat her down gently and she sat beside her. 'You see,' she began. 'health workers are people who are trained to provide healthcare for people. There are doctors, nurses, pharmacists and others. Doctors are the ones who administer the treatment and prescribed the drugs, nurses assist the doctor to administer the treatment and pharmacists tell the patient how to use their drugs.' Sharon hoped her explanation was basic enough for her.
'Which one of professions are you?'
Sharon was glad she understood her. She smiled and held her on the shoulder. 'I'm a doctor.'
'Did you give my mother drugs? My father couldn't cure her with herbs until you came.'
Sharon nodded. She needed no one to tell her that the little girl's mum was one of those who had been cured of the deadly flu. 'Well, yes. I did prescribe some drugs for her.'
'Will my mother be sick again?' Her tone changed from inquisition to worry.
'No,' Sharon answered. 'If she takes her drugs as directed, then she'll never fall sick again.'
If Beauty was convinced by her answer, she didn't show it. 'Can I be a doctor like you when I grow up so I can treat my mother when she falls sick?'
Sharon nodded as she lifted her up and sat her down on her laps. 'Yes, my dear. You can be whatever you want to be. You can be a doctor, a nurse or a pharmacist. Just study your books well.'

That was the day Beauty made up her mind to become a doctor. She started following her passion and made it clear to anyone who cared to listen that she wanted to become a medical doctor when she was grown. Her teachers knew she had what it took academically. She was always top of her class. What bothered them was the finance and not until when she had to drop out of secondary school while in senior school one, they never stopped doubting her abilities.

Beauty was jerked back to reality by sudden streak of lightning. She held her tray with her right hand and managed to look up. She was astonished to see that the clouds had turned dark. Rain was impending and with the rumbles of thunders that preceded the lightning, she knew the rain was inevitable. She hadn't sold all her wares, but her mother had told her that anytime it was about to rain, she must always return home. With unrestrained force, she kicked the polyethylene terephthalate bottle one last time and headed the shortest route to her house. The bottle skidded off the road and landed on a duck and her ducklings playing heartily in a nearby gutter. The duck and her duckling quacked and dispersed to safety.
'Sorry!' Beauty muttered to them as she hurried along. 'I didn't intend to hurt you.'

The sky continued rumbling as Beauty doubled her pace. The mass of cloud high above had clustered into a wholly mountain and was accompanied by the flashes of lightning and roars of thunders. There was a mini pandemonium. Men and woman, young and old scampered hastily for safety from the rain. Store owners packed their wares and shut their stores swiftly and mothers grabbed their children and hurried along. Everyone was scampering to avoid been drenched by the obviously impending rain. Beauty got home just in time before the heavens opened and poured down its content.

Her younger siblings were at hand to welcome her. It was obvious that they had been playing football in the dusty ground in front of their house. Her siblings were all boys and all but the youngest one had stopped schooling as well. Samuel was fifteen, he was taller than Beauty and appeared older than his age. Most of the time, he helped their mother on the farm. He was quite an intelligent lad and did not take dropping out of school to be bad as Beauty had taken it. He seemed to understand perfectly the situation at hand despite his young age and was always willing to help. Their mother had promised them that they would return to school as soon as things get better as she was saving up part of their earnings to ensure that. While Beauty looked forward to the day she would return to school with anticipation, Samuel was indifferent. He didn't mind staying away from school if it meant they would have something to eat. To him, there was no point in going to school on an empty stomach.

Matip was the third child. A twelve-year-old boy who knew better than to complain whenever he didn't have enough to eat. He knew his mother would give him more if there was more. He was always eager to follow his mother and brother to the farm, but his mother was always hesitant to take him along. Although she could do with his help, Matip's inquisitive nature and clumsiness worked well against him most of the time. Like Samuel, he didn't care much about being in school, but he hung up to the hope of returning to school one day. Seeing his friends in the neighborhood going to school always made him feel bad and left behind and this fueled his desire to follow his mother to the farm.

Joel, nine, was the last child and the only one they could afford to continue sending to school. He was only a toddler when their father died. Beauty loved him and pampered him more than the others. She was quite envious of him because he had what she coveted most. Although she was happy that he was in school, she wished she was in school as well. Her hopes of returns to school seemed to fade away with every passing day. Every time she dares to raise the topic of returning to school with her mom, she always got the same response she got years ago when she had first dropped out of school. Beauty usually replayed the memories of that of that hot summer night with tears.

She was on the mat outside their compound, doing her assignments silently while her brothers played around under the moonlight. The heat during the summer could not be equated, hence almost all family in the town had made a habit of staying outside late at night to enjoy fresh air before they finally went into sleep. Occasionally, when she was disturbed by their hearty noise, she would raise her head and order them to quit playing around. Her orders usually last only few minutes after she had given them but the moment her focus goes back to her assignment, they start disturbing her again.

'Stop playing around!' She would say. 'Can't you all just sit quietly in a place?' The boys would comport themselves and remain quiet while the reprimand lasted. 'It's late already, so just saved your plays for another day.'

'But Beauty, we are done with our school assignments ...'

'Shhhhh!' She interrupted as one of them tried to protest, placing a finger across her lips in her trademark move. 'I didn't ask for your opinion Samuel. And what if you're done with your homework? Don't you know you have to study hard to pass your exams and come out top of your class?' The boys fell silent and after a moment, she resumed her assignments.

About five minutes later, she was ordering them again to stop playing. 'All of you will never listen to me!' She snapped. 'Now go in and bring your homework let me see what you have done.'

All three boys grudgingly went into the house to do as they were told.

Her mother came out just as the boys went in. She sat beside her on the mat. 'Beauty,' she said, placing her hand on her shoulder and gently massaging it. 'Why not leave your brothers and allow them play?'

Beauty turned to face her mother. 'You know how naughty your boys can be...' She stopped midway as they heard a lounge crash sound coming from the house.'

'Samuel what is it?' Their mother asked, raised her voice a bit to ensure he heard her from the inside.

'Nothing Mother, Matip slipped but he's fine.' Samuel answered.

Any worries she had about Matip being injured vanished as a loud roar of laughter emanated from the house. Matip dashed out, followed by Samuel both laughing heartily. Little Joel was far behind them, unable to keep up with their pace. They dashed back as fast as they dashed out.

'You see, mother? They play too much. I sent them in to fetch their homework for me to see and all they could do is to resume their play back in the house.'

Queen smiled. 'You worry too much about these children,' she said as she intensified the massage. They will grow off it. If you were a boy, I bet you would be playing around with them as well.'

Beauty stiffened a smile. 'I'm happy that I am not a boy. I can't imagine myself playing around and not taking my studies serious.'

Queen managed to force a smile. 'Speaking about your studies, my beloved,' she fondly referred to her as my beloved. She took her hand off her shoulder and moved to her hair, playing with it gently. Beauty loved it when she played with her hair. She loved her mother and she knew she loved them as well. Even though there was no help forthcoming from any family member, she was doing her best ensure that are children were well provided for. However, it seemed her best was no longer enough. A long silence followed and after what seemed like an eternity, beauty broke it with a question.

'What about my studies Mother? I'm still doing quite well, I'm top of my class and all my teachers like me. Did anyone of them tell you anything?'

'No, my beloved. I know you're doing so well in school and I'm truly proud of you. Which makes it even more painful for me to break this to you.'

Beauty could tell that she was trying to hide her tears. She sat up and held her hand. 'What is it mother?' She asked. 'Why are you crying?'

'You'll have to forgive me for this Beauty,' she replied. 'If there was someone who knew how important education was to Beauty, then it was her. She knew she was going to be devastated, she will most likely cry, she would be down for days. But her hands were tied. If there was somewhat, she could do to make sure this didn't happen, then she would have done it without hesitation. 'I want you to understand that I value your education as much as you value it. But since your father died, it has been very difficult for me to take care of you and your siblings.'

'I know Mother, I understand, and I appreciate you for all you do. Could you however stop beating around the bush and go straight to the point or whatever is making you cry?'

'You'll have to stop schooling for the meantime.' Queen swallowed hard on her saliva as she dropped the bombshell.

Beauty sank to the floor as the effects of the bombshell settled agonizingly on her. Tears swelled up in her eyes in an instant. 'Does this mean I can't go to school anymore?' She asked with teary eyes.'

'No, my beloved, it only means you can't go to school any more this term. Your teacher was here this afternoon. She politely told me not to allow you come to school until you pay your fees, because the school was planning on sending the pupils who have not paid their school fees back home tomorrow.'

'When will I return to school?'

'As soon as things get better my beloved. I'm already planning to start saving up so that you can return to school next term.'

'What about my brothers?'

'They'll continue going to school as long as they're not sent out of school. If they are, then Samuel might have to join me on the farm.' She watched in pains as the tears streamed down her young daughter's cheeks. 'Listen my beloved,' she continued. 'I would not want you to stay at home idle. One of my friends have agreed to sell some fishes for me on credit. Tomorrow I'll smoke them, and you can hawk them in the evening. From there we'll have more money to feed ourselves and save up for your schooling.'

The deal seems fair to her. She understands the pains that her mother was passing through and she didn't want to compound them by not being understanding. 'Mother,' she said, wiping her tears with the back of her right palm. 'I understand you and I know that you have my best interest at heart. I will go to school tomorrow and the day after tomorrow until I am sent out of school. The day I am sent out of school, I will start helping you to hawk the smoked fish.'

'It's alright my beloved. If that is what you want. I will hawk the fish myself tomorrow, and then the day after tomorrow and every day if need be.' She patted her on the back before she got up and went inside. Beauty's notebooks were the recipient of the hot tears that streamed down her face the moment her mother left.

Beauty watched with a smile on her face as her siblings played around in the rain. Moments earlier, the boys had tried to welcome her with an embrace, but she had shorn them off due to how dirty they were. Even Joel didn't get his trademark hug as she deemed him too dirty as well. On enquiry, she was told that their mother wasn't back from the market yet. While she went in to get something to eat, the boys ran back outside as the rain descended in heavy torrents. She dished her food and went to the door, food in her hand, watching her brothers kick a football around aimlessly under the rain, they looked happy doing it, and she wished for the umpteenth time, that she could go back to school soon enough. Only that could give her the happiness that she truly carved.

She however knew that was not going to happen anytime soon. They could barely afford two meals a day and even the sales of smoked fish have been poor these past weeks. Despite her efforts to enhance sales, she realized that there is more competition as some other children in the town had begun hawking smoked fish as well. Promiscuous men here and there were promising to patronize her if only she would get intimate with them. Beauty stayed away from such men, she was not in any way going to sell her dignity for the sales of a few smoked fish or anything else for that matter. She would never disappoint God or her mother.

She remembered that there was little water left in the house and she dashed inside to fetch their rubber buckets which she placed at the end of their roof so that the water dripping off the roof could drop inside. When she had done this, she finished up her meal and returned to the house to calculate the sales she made for the day. The rain showed no sign of slowing down. Neither did her brothers.

CHAPTER TWO

THE sun was shining high up the sky. The hazy harmattan morning had gradually been replaced by a scorching sun and a bright day. People went about their business in the normal fashion at the town's market. Although, the day wasn't very busy for the marketers because it wasn't the market day. Activities in the market were always frenzy on market days. The market would be overcrowded with people and all shops stocked filled with goods.

Some shop owners were wetting the ground around their shops with water to reduce the effects of the dusts.

Some were using hand towels to wipe the dusts off their goods. Buyers moved from one point of the market to another while sellers try to entice them by advertising their different goods. Queen walked through the narrow paths in the market. On this day, she was neither a buyer nor a seller. She had in fact come to see one of her most trusted friends who had called to inform her the previous day that they needed to discuss something of high importance. She had immediately assured her that she would come and see her at her stall in the market the next day. As she wriggled her way to her friend's stall, she wondered what the discussion could be about. Surely none of her children had fermented trouble whatsoever. She knew them better than anybody else. She trained them well and brought them up the right way. To her, poverty was no excuse for failing to bring up a child in the proper way.

Ude, as her friend was popular called was a mother of four herself. But unlike her, her children were grown up and all but one of them were living in the city and they regularly sent stipends to their mother. Ude brought up her children well as well. She and Queen had grown up together, although she got married some five or six years before Queen. Her husband was late as well, but fortunately he left a couple of properties and cash behind for her. With this, life was relatively easier for her. Ude had no doubt been a very supportive friend to Queen. She was the one who advised her to allow her Beauty hawk smoked fish instead of remaining idle while they gathered money for her to return to school. Since she herself sold frozen fish, it was easy for her to give her a portion to smoke and sell.

Queen thought she was summoned because she had not remitted the money from the fish sales to her for the past two weeks. She braced up her mind on how to deal if that should be the reason why she summoned her. She got to her stall and met her attending to some customers. They exchanged warm pleasantries and Queen proceeded to sit on one of the two stools in the store while she waited for her to finish attending to her customers. When she was done, she offered her a sachet of cold water which she collected thankfully and gulped down at once. The scorching sun had no doubt had a devastating effect on her and increased her craving for water.
'Ude,' she began, deciding that it will be better to raise the issue herself. 'I'm really sorry I've not remitted any money to you for the past two weeks. Sales have been really poor.'
Ude smiled. 'Do you think that is the reason that I called you here?'
Queen nodded slowly.
'You're wrong Queen. Your assumption is wrong. We've known each other since childhood and we've been doing this business together for several years now, so why would I be bothered that you haven't remitted any money to me for two weeks?'
'I assumed it was because of that...'
'You don't assume Queen. You should have asked me why I called you. The reason I want to see you is far more important than the remittance of two-week sales money.'
'I'm sorry Ude.'
'You better be. Sales have been poor here as well, so I understand. People are lamenting that there is no money in the economy. There is recession and naira keep crashing against the dollar. There isn't much we can do about it yet. You see those people you met when you got here?' Queen nodded and she continued. 'They are my very good and loyal customers. Until last week, they've never bought anything from me on credit for years. I wasn't even shocked; I understand the situation and I really felt for them. The government owe workers several months of unpaid salary.'
If there was anything Queen loved most about Ude, it was her understanding and generous nature, countless times she had come to the rescue of her and the children when it appeared like they were going to starve to death. She gave willingly and without hesitation and Queen was glad to have been blessed with a friend like her. 'Thank you,' she replied. 'I promise to remit as soon as sales improve.'

'Don't worry about that Queen. Don't let that bother you. How are your children?'

'They are all fine. Thank you.'

'Glory to God. Now let's get straight to the point. Have you seen your daughter recently?'

Queen's forehead creased into vertical lines. Seen Beauty recently? They slept and woke up together every day! 'I don't understand you,' she finally said.

'Queen! You are a woman. You should understand what I meant by that. I mean, have you noticed how your daughter have grown into a very beautiful and matured lady?'

Queen smiled, more at her own ignorance than at what she said. 'Of course, I know. We share the same roof. Beautiful lady, no doubt about that. But matured, I have my reservations. Beauty is just seventeen.'

'Age has nothing to do with maturity. She is grown. Physically she is matured and ready to be harvested. I look at her a lot whenever she comes here. I must admit she certainly is the envy of so many girls of her age. Her breasts are plump and full, and she definitely has the body of one of these movie stars...Ermmm, what's her name again?' She paused momentarily; her right hand suspended in the air in a bid to remember the name. 'Omotola! Omotola Jolade! Men would be dying to have her as their wife.'

'What exactly are you insinuating Ude?' All what she heard her say appeared to her like a puzzle that needed to be solved. First, she thought that Beauty was probably pregnant. But she ruled that out because she knew her daughter better than anyone else. If Beauty was pregnant, then she would be the first person to know.

'Be patient Queen, I'll get there shortly.'

'Alright.'

'Do you know Wemi?'

Queen racked her brain to recollect the named. Ude helped her out. 'Wemi is the second wife of Chief Frederick. That Chief who married so many wives and later ran away with a white woman about ten years ago'

'Oh yes! I remainder,' she said as the memories came flooding back to her. 'Wemi moved to the city when her first child went to America some years ago. We've not heard from her since then.'

'Yes exactly! I saw Wemi three days ago.'

'Oh, really?'

'Yes. I tell you she looks far better than when she left for the city.'

'I can imagine. She's living in the city and her son in America is sending her dollars regularly. Life doesn't get any better.'

'You're right. Well, she talked to me about so many things including her son, Felix in America. He wants to come home in some months' time and she wants him to get married before returning. She said he's long overdue for marriage.'

'Oh...is he that old? I thought men can always get married at any time.'

'Not really. Felix is thirty-five.'

'Oh...he's really overdue for marriage.'

'Yes, and that was the major reason why she came. She wants a wife for him, and she wants a lady from our town here.'

'Now I see where you are going,' Queen replied.

'Listen to me. I didn't just arrive at the decision of choosing Beauty for him. I carefully screened all the young ladies in this town, and I arrived at the conclusion that Beauty is not only the most beautiful among them, she is the most intelligent and well behaved among the lot. I have no doubt that Felix and her mother will like her.'

'For the love of Christ Ude, Beauty is just seventeen! And moreover, I still have plans to return her of school very soon.' Queen protested.

'Seventeen? And you said you've seen her recently? I was seventeen when I got married, you know right? Beauty is matured for marriage. And you talk about school? It is over three years now since she had dropped out of school, how much have you been able to save towards her education?' Queen shook her head pathetically and Ude continued, 'Nothing Queen, nothing. Instead, her brothers also have to drop out in that period as well. Be realistic with yourself. How long is she going to hawk smoked fish for you while you keep fueling her pipe dream of returning to school with unrealistic promise and fake savings?' She stopped to let the effects of her words settle on her.

Queen knew she was right. But how could she give her daughter away in marriage to a stranger who was eighteen whole years older than her? 'Have you considered that Felix is eighteen years older than Beauty?'

'Age is nothing but numbers Queen. I expected you to be smarter than this. Don't let me down.'

'But Beauty,' she said, tears starting to assemble in her eyes. 'The only thing she wants is to go to school and become a medical doctor.'

'Who said she won't go to school and become a medical doctor? Felix will send her to school and help her realize her dream of becoming a medical doctor. The money you'll get from the bride price that will be paid for her would be enough for you to send her siblings back to school and start the clothing business that you've always dreamt of. This is an opportunity presented to you on a platter of gold and it does not come around every day. Do you want to live in lack and want for the rest of your life?'

Queen was lost in a chain of thoughts for a long time. This was truly an opportunity presented on a platter of gold. An opportunity to turn her life and that of her children around for the better. 'Alright. I've agreed on my path. But I'll still need to talk to my daughter about it and seek her consent.'

'Good! I assure you that you would not regret this. Talk to your daughter and make her see reasons why this is good for her, for you and for her siblings as well. I already told Wemi about her and she seemed to like her. However, I told her I will speak with you about it. Now that you have consented to it. I'll happily let her know.'

'Alright Ude. Thank you so much. I must be on my way now. I haven't been to the farm in some days.'

'Relax, Queen. Once everything clicks, you will neither to stress yourself nor the children over the farm again. Felix might even take Beauty with him back to America. I'm sure once he sees how beautiful she is he wouldn't want to spend a minute without her.'

Queen managed to force a smile.

'Trust me, I want nothing but the best for you and your children and I would not push you into any harm. Let me know as soon as you've discussed it with her.'

Queen stood up as she prepared to leave. Ude stood as well and she squeezed some naira notes into her hand. 'Here. Buy some bread for your children.'

Queen thanked her heartily and left just as some customers arrived at the stall. Her head was filled with plenty of thoughts as she made her way back home. She would not be going to the farm after all, she had plenty of things to think about. And most imperative of all, knowing how emotional her daughter was, she had some serious convincing to do.

CHAPTER THREE

QUEEN sighed for the umpteenth time that night. It was drizzling lightly, and the strokes of the rain could be heard on their roof. A cricket was chirping in the dimly lit room. Queen was seated on the edge of the bed. Her eyes hovered from the lamp to her children who were fast asleep and oblivious of their mother's state. Her eyes stopped at the figure of Beauty who stirred simultaneously. What fate would befall her daughter? How will she take the news of her impending marriage? Would she see reasons why it was best that she got married and agree to it? These and many more questions plagued her heart. Even her bad never met the supposed groom. How was she supposed to give her daughter away in marriage to someone she herself had never met? Would he take care of her? She knew my agreeing to the marriage she was taking a huge gamble, one that all she could hope for was that it paid off. Perhaps things could have been different if her husband was alive. Tears streamed down without restrain from her face.

Beauty stirred in bed again and this time, she caught glimpse of her mother seated on the edge of the bed. She rubbed her eyes slowly with the back of her right hand and sat up. Queen noticed she was awake and cleaned the tears of her eyes immediately.
'Why are you not asleep mother?' She asked amidst yawning, sleep still prevalent in her eyes.
'I just woke up to ease myself,' she lied. 'Go back to sleep.'
Beauty stood up and sat beside her. 'That's not true mother. I've been hearing sighs and sobs in my sleep. You've been crying.' She bent and raised the lamp on the bedside table to her face. 'I knew it. You've been crying mum. What is the matter? What's bothering you?'
'Really, Beauty it's nothing to worry about. Please go back to sleep.' She replied, turning away from her.
'If anything is enough to make you cry, then it's something to worry about. Please tell me mother, what is it?'
Queen sighed again. 'I know your dream has always been to become a medical doctor,' she began. 'But what if I'm unable to get the money required to send you back to school?'
'Please don't say that. I believe God will make a way where there is no way. You know, the bible makes us to understand that eyes have not seen, ears have not heard, and it hasn't even entered the earth of men, the things that God has planned for those that love him. I don't want you to be bothered over this issue. God will definitely not abandon us-we are his people.'
Queen forced a smile, amazed by the young girl's show of faith. She sighed again. 'What if God has already made a way?'
'I don't understand mum. Which way is that?'
'I mean since it hasn't entered into our heart what plan God has for us, what if God has made a way but it is not the kind of way, we thought he would make that he made?'
Beauty shifted uneasily. 'Can you please go straight to the point mother? The suspense is killing me.'
'My beloved. I want you to know that I have your best interest at heart. You're my daughter and I would not want anything bad to happen to you. I would not have agreed to this if I wasn't sure it was the best thing for you, your siblings and for me. You know, since your father died, things have been extremely difficult for us. But someone is here to change that now.'

'I understand mother. Now who is this person that God has sent to change our status?'

'His name is Felix. He lives in America.'

'Does he want to marry me?'

Queen should have known that her daughter was smart enough to decode what was on ground. 'Yes, my beloved. Her mother has asked for your hand in marriage on behalf of him.'

'But you know I want to return to school, not get married. And yet you call this God's way?' By this time, she was fighting to hold back her tears. 'This is not God's way mother; this is your way.'

'Don't say that my beloved. This is not my plan at all. And you are wrong. The young man is willing to take care of you and send you to school. Getting married does not stop you from achieving your dream especially when your husband is more than willing to support your dreams.' She paused, allowing the effects of her words to sink in on her.

Beauty was silent. She bowed her head in serious consideration of what her mother just said. Perhaps it was truly her best way to achieve her dreams. Her mother clearly lacked the financial means to return her to school dealt her best efforts. But she hadn't seen this man. What if she doesn't like him or he doesn't like her? What if she reneges on his promises, maltreat her and refuse to send her to school after their marriage? There were a lot of questions begging her for answers. But it appeared like only time could answer her if she agreed.

'Beauty,' her mother continued. 'You should know I would never want anything bad for you. Think about it. You will return to school, your brothers will return to school, I won't have to work like a slave under the sun anymore and Every one of us would be happy. Ude even told me that he might take you back with him to America. Don't you want to go to America?'

It was Beauty's turn to sigh. 'But mother, what if he doesn't like me?'

'My beloved, have you seen yourself in the mirror? You're so beautiful and every man would want to have you as their wife. That is not a possibility at all.'

'What if I don't like him?'

'You will my dear. He's a young man doing well, and you will learn to please him and like him.'

'How old is he Mother?'

Queen knew the questions would come in fast and thick and she was more than prepared to answer them. However, she made up her mind to tell her the truth no matter how difficult it is. 'He is thirty-five. But you see age is just mere numbers when it comes to...'

'Thirty-five!' Beauty's jaws fell open, unable to contain her shock. 'Mother that's eighteen whole years older than I am.'

'Yes, my beloved. But age doesn't matter. If you love each other. Age is just mere numbers. You see, my father was twenty-one years older than my mother. But they lived happily until my father passed away at the ripe age of eighty-one. Age does not matter my daughter.'

Beauty appeared to think about it for a while. 'Have you met him? Is he a good man?' She finally asked after a silence that appeared to last for ages.

'To be honest, I haven't met him, and I can't say if he's a good man or not. But my friend, Ude told me so many things about him and I'm convinced. You know Ude is our benefactor and I don't think she would want to harm us for any reason. If he is a bad man, she would have told me.'

'What if he reneged on his promises and refuses to send me to school?'

'He definitely will. Ude assured me of that. Like I said earlier, Ude told me that he might even take you back with him to America. When you get there, you will see plenty white men and you can be going to school and sending us dollars.

The thought of going to America and living a better life appealed to Beauty. She was no longer crying but in deep thoughts. She hoped everything would work out as smoothly as her mother had painted it. She could not even imagine things going wrong. She wanted to realize her dream of becoming a medical doctor and

bringing her family out of poverty. So, if that means getting married at her tender age, then she would not mind. She prayed that God's will be done. 'It's alright mother. I hope everything goes as anticipated though.' Queen gave her a warm hug. 'By God's grace my beloved. Everything is going to be alright.'
Beauty sighed. Amen, she said silently.

~~~~   ~~~~   ~~~~   ~~~~

Queen's compound was riddled with a beehive of activities. The day was finally set of Beauty's engagements to Felix. It had been a day the two families had been waiting for. Ude was obviously excited as she gave orders to men who were offloading tubers of yam and other items such as crates of soft drinks into the house. Queen was in the room with some other women, getting Beauty ready for arguably the biggest day of her life. As much as she had looked forward to this day, her excitement was deflated when she was told the previous day that her husband to be would not be in the country for their engagement. This initially threw both queen and beauty off balance. Wemi, the groom's mother, had explained to them that her son had had difficulty securing the necessary paper works needed to return to the country for the engagement and had offered them the options of postponing engagement in order to give him more time to secure the necessary travelling paper works or sending Beauty over to America after the engagement and they would get married there. She explained that should they agree to allow the engagement to proceed, Felix would send them the visa and ticket fees to enable her to join him in America as soon as possible.

Even though Queen was initially skeptical about both arrangements, Ude had convinced her that it was an opportunity for her daughter to travel abroad since her would be husband would be covering all necessary expenses. She advised that she allowed the engagement to proceed in the absence of her would be husband. Queen agreed and managed to convince Beauty even though she had her reservations.
Queen met with Wemi and discussed with her over them waiting until Beauty was eighteen years before they got married. Wemi had no issues with it. Beauty was about nine months to her eighteenth birthday and Wemi assured her that they would wait. Queen also told her that she wanted her daughter to stay in a convent until after their wedding due to their religious beliefs and Wemi promised to ensure that all her wishes were honored.

Beauty's siblings were excited as well. They had pummeled her with various questions relating to her marriage and if she will still go to school. She had patiently answered all their questions and assured them that she would take good care of them. As she was being dressed that morning, tears of uncertainty streamed down her cheeks. She didn't know for certain what would become of her after the marriage. However, she kept her hopes high. She had taken the news of her groom being unable to make it for their engagement in good fate, embracing the positivity of going to America right after the engagement. In her thoughts, going to America was a way to bring her family out of poverty and realize her dreams. Although it still felt odd to her that her engagement would be held in her fiancé's absence.

Her uncertainty was clothed in further doubt when she traveled to visit a famous prophet two weeks earlier. She had discussed visiting the popular prophet in the neighboring state with her mother and although she was skeptical about it at first-on the premise of it being against their catholic faith-but when Beauty had insisted on hearing from a man of God. What God has to say about her impending marriage, she had eventually, albeit reluctantly given her blessings to go see the prophet.

Beauty would soon find out that going to see a popular prophet without a prior appointment could be costly. When she arrived at the church, she was told that the prophet was out of the state and would not be returning until the next day. Without having anywhere to stay, she begged them that they allow her to pass the night in the church. That night, she slept on the cold floors of the church, eating some of the bread her mother gave
~~~~

her for the trip. The next day when the prophet arrived, she was told by his secretary that he would only attend to those who had a prior appointment. She was devastated. All her pleadings and explanations fell on deaf ears although she could stay for the night in the church again. The next day, after much pleading with the secretary, she was eventually given an appointment for the next day. However, by the next day, she was told that the prophet had an emergency and had to travel out of the state urgently. Beauty was devastated beyond words. She contemplated returning but after remembering how much effort it took her to convince her mother to allow her to visit the prophet, she decided to stay.

Feeding proved to be a huge challenge for her as she had already depleted all her feeding provisions by this time. She never planned to stay if she did. Her plan was to see the prophet and return home at most the next day. The only money she had left on her was her transport fare back home. She had to beg the secretary for some money to feed after she explained her predicament. The secretary reluctantly gave her some money. Finally, the prophet returned from his urgent trip and luck smiled on her and she was eventually able to see him so much to her relief and delight.

'Come in,' a thin voice said in response to the knock Beauty planted on the door. She opened the door slowly and stepped into the prophet's office. Prophet Elano was a well-known prophet. Famous for his prophecies and miracles in the state and neighboring states. Beauty wasn't sure what to expect. She however made up her mind to accept anything she got.
'God afternoon sir,' she greeted as she stepped in, managing to steady her shaky feet.
'Young lady, good afternoon. Please have your sit.' He gestured to a chair in front of his desk. The pastor is a tall, muscular man with fair complexion and clean-shaven beards that was in contrast with his mini afro hair. He appeared like a man in his early fifties. Beauty thought he was much younger than she anticipated him to be.
'Thank you, sir,' she replied as sat as instructed. Beauty gave a cursory glance around the office. Two giant portraits of the prophet hang on the wall behind his desk. There was a huge bookshelf to her right. The lower part contained various books which she suspected that at least most of them were Christian books. The upper part of the shelf contained various award plaques and trophies.
'I heard you've wanted to see me for quite a while,' the prophet's thin voice rang out, jerking her back from her mini trance.
'Ye...ss sir,' she stammered. 'I'm sorry; I was a bit carried away.'
'It's alright. Most people can't help it the first time they step into this office. There's an aura, a force that compels them to marvel.' Beauty merely shook her head; she wasn't sure what to say. The prophet continued.
"What is your name?'
'Beauty,' she replied. 'Benjamin Beauty sir.'
'I would bet your friends call you BB?'
Beauty managed a smile and nodded. 'You are right sir.' She shifted uneasily in her chair. There was a look on the prophet's face that told her he found her attractive. That wasn't the problem, every man found her attractive. The problem was that he kept licking his lips every now and then like someone who was about to devour a plate of sumptuous meal. She couldn't tell if that was how he acted at all time or if he was just acting like that with her. She decided not to assume and be as norms and straightforward with him as much as she could.
'Let us pray,' he said. Beauty closed her eyes and the prophet led a prayer that lasted for about seven minutes. She was pleased when it was finally over but to her shock, the prophet was by now, sitting on the desk directly opposite to her instead of the chair where he was when the prayers began. The thoughts of the man having ulterior motives came to her mind and she banished it immediately. Prophet Elano was a popular and well-respected man of God and he would not attempt to take advantage of his hapless followers. She silently

said a prayer of forgiveness for suspecting God's servant as he spoke.

'You're here because of your impending marriage,' he said.

'Yes sir. How did you know that?' Beauty could not hide her amazement.

'The Lord told me during the prayer. You want to be certain if he is the right man for you.'

'Yes sir. I'm seriously confused.' She went ahead and explained everything to him in full details.

'The good Lord has shown me everything. Even the ones you didn't remember to tell me. The Lord told me during the prayer that that man is not your husband. You have to cancel the engagement and other wedding plans.'

Beauty shifted in her chair. 'He isn't my husband?'

'Yes, my daughter,' he said, moving closer to her as he spoke. He ran his hand through her hair and Beauty was taken aback. She politely removed his hand from her hair and shifted her chair backwards. 'Look here Beauty,' he continued. 'Don't be sacred. That man does not have the means to take care of you. He is an illegal migrant in America who does not even have a work permit. All people like him do is to ride taxis at night to earn a living so they won't get caught and be sent back to Nigeria.'

Beauty sighed. She was completely lost in thoughts. First her intended husband was not God's choice for her and second, the prophet was trying to sexually assault her-confirming her initial fears of him. I was right, she said silently to herself. Oh Lord, I take back my prayers of forgiveness.'

Standing up from the table, he said, 'You are just as beautiful as your name, young woman.' He stood beside her and caressed her face. 'You are beautiful, and prefect and I would bet touching you would be so nice.

Beauty felt irritated. She watched in disgust as he licked his lips for the umpteenth time. 'I thought you were a true man of God,' she said. 'I almost can't believe you are doing this.'

The prophet paused. 'You don't have to be rude young woman. What does been a man of God have to do with admiring the wonderful work of God?'

'Shame on you Prophet Elano. Hiding behind God's words to perpetrate unholy things.' She stood up to leave but he held her back and attempted to kiss her. Beauty was smart enough to dodge his kiss and wriggle away from his grip. He grabbed her again and this time, tried to pin her down. Beauty let out a scream that caught him unaware. He tried to cover her mouth, but she screamed more loudly. Realizing that he could not get the better of her he freed her from his grip.

'We will surely meet again,' he said, breathing heavily as a result of the struggle with her. 'And next time we meet there would be no escaping!'

Beauty was too dumbfounded to reply. She dashed out through the door without thinking twice or looking back. She had just escaped from the hands of a sexual predator that people referred to as a prophet.

As she returned home, all her thoughts were occupied with what the prophet told her and how he tried to sexually molest her. She was relieved that she managed to escape and wondered how many ladies like her were unfortunate not to escape the raging hormones of a man widely regarded as a famous prophet. He had categorically told him that Felix was not her husband, but was she to believe the word of a prophet cum sexual predator? If what he said about Felix not being her husband was true, then he had cast doubt into his own words by sexually harassing her. If what he said wasn't true, then he wanted her for keeps due to his own selfish interest. She concluded she could not believe the words of such a prophet even if she wanted to. Then there was the problem of her family. Her mother was looking up to her to become the breadwinner of the family and lift them out of their extreme poverty. If she believes the words of the prophet and refused to marry Felix, her mother would be so disappointed with her. If she dares went back on the marriage, she will put her family to shame and turn them to laughingstock in the community as the engagement had already been fixed. She could not afford to let her mother down or put her own future on the line due to the words of a randy prophet. She therefore decided to keep what happened and what the prophet said to herself and bear the risk of marrying Felix. It was worth the risk, she thought. If it worked out well, fine. If it didn't work out well, then she hoped the prophet would not have the last laugh. They would never meet again.

Beauty fought back tears as she was led outside to meet her husband's family. There were about five canopies in their compound and all of them were filled with guests and family members. Under one of the canopies were the things that the husband had brought for her. They ranged from yam to drinks to clothing materials and other provisions and accessories. She glanced at her mother who was seated under a canopy to her right and saw that she was trying to fight back tears of her own. That intensified her tears, but she wiped them away almost immediately. She saw her siblings going from one place to another. They were obviously excited, but Beauty was certain that they were oblivious of the magnitude of what was at hand. There were loud claps and cheers from all present as she stepped under the canopy provided for the bride and groom. The drummers displayed their skills and she was urged to dance to the huge chair prepared for her. Beauty glanced at her in-laws under their own canopy and forced a smile.
She sighed, accepting her fate in good faith.

CHAPTER FOUR

It had been over two months since Beauty got engaged to Felix. The engagement had been a success and although wasn't as huge as some people expected of a groom who stays in America, nevertheless it still sent tongues wagging in positive directions. There was plenty to eat and drink for everyone who attended courtesy of the husband's family. It was a day Beauty would always remember with a smile and save for the fact that her husband was not present; she had no reason not to be happy about how things had panned out.

Over the two months that followed, her mother had obtained a small stall in the market where she sold various clothing materials and she no longer go to the farm. She leased out the farm to someone who paid her on a monthly basis. Samuel and Matip had returned to school much to Beauty's delight. She was glad that she decided to marry Felix as her decision was already paying off. She never thought that things would turn around in such a short period of time. She was beginning to hope again and have faith in the future. Things were going to be alright, she believed.

It was however after the engagement that Beauty began to encounter her first challenge. True to their promise, Felix had sent money to Queen to enable Beauty to obtain her international passport and visa so that she could join him there. First, it took about two weeks for her international passport to be ready. Then there came the difficulty in obtaining a visa as her application was declined. It was a trying period for her. She thought of the consequences of the visa not being granted. Queen continued to encourage her to look at the bright side of things. Beauty was optimistic. She continued to pray and did not let her faith fade in the face of the challenges. It became more difficult for her to keep up to her faith when her application was declined the second time. Wemi reminded them that it was just the second month and there was still about seven months before she was eighteen. She urged them not to give up. She even took Beauty to the market and brought her new clothes for her impending trip.

Beauty and Queen were buoyed by her kind words and acts. It made Beauty even more determined to be granted the visa. She had had two visa interviews under her belt, and she was quite confident that it would be a case of third time luck for her. She put in for the visa the third time and hoped that it would at last come out successful. On the day of the interview, she prayed and asked God to take over.
The interview went like the previous two she had. She was asked series of questions which she answered to the best of her knowledge. This time however, one of Ude's sons' friend who was visiting from the city had given her some tips few days to the interview. Charmed with these tips, she was able to successfully navigate the tricky questions thrown at her.

A couple of weeks after the interview, she received the news that she had been granted a four-year visa with great joy and excitement. There was jubilation in their house. Her mother was as excited as Beauty herself was. Her brothers were ecstatic because they thought it meant their sister would always send them dollars. Ude and Wemi and the rest of the family and other well wishers were relieved and excited at the same time. It was finally time for the young bride to go and meet her husband. Beauty knew she wouldn't be seeing her mother or siblings for quite some time. She found herself relapsing into a skeptical young lady who was going to a country where she had never been and was getting married to a man, she had never met but only seen in pictures that Ude had shown her and her mother. Things had been going quite well till this stage, and she thought that if it was any indication of what to expect, then she was definitely in good hands. Her husband's family had been extremely kind to her. Wemi had given her all her support and encouraged her whenever she felt down. She couldn't pray for a better mother in-law. She hoped things would remain smooth till the end, but she was a smart lady and she understood that life wasn't a bed of roses. More challenges will later arise, but one thing she was certain of, was that with her mother and mother in-law, and most importantly, with God on her side, she would not lack the will to fight those challenges to a standstill.

The set day for Beauty's departure to the United States of America finally arrived at unquenchable excitement for everyone related to her. Her mother, her siblings Ude and Wemi were all on hand to see her off to the airline. Tears flowed without restrains as the plane ran through the runways. For Beauty, it was the beginning of a new journey in her life; one that she hoped will bring her dreams to fruition and help her family out of poverty. For her mother however, she hoped things went according to plans and that her daughter was in the right hands. It had been difficult marrying off her daughter to a complete stranger and she could only pray that her decision didn't come back to haunt her. Things had been going on well so far and the least she could hope for was that things continued to go on smoothly and her daughter achieves her dreams. The thoughts of not seeing her daughter for some years brought more tears to her eyes.

After several hours of an exhausting flight, Beauty finally touched down in America. It was an experience that she would never forget in a hurry. She stood at the airport arrivals after undergoing all necessarily checks and waited anxiously to meet her groom. This was a man she had got engaged to without even meeting. She didn't really know what he looked like; neither did he know what she looked like. Many questions began flooding her mind. What if she didn't like him? Or what if he didn't like her? Would he be looking too old for him? She tried not to worry too much about everything, but she could not help herself. She thought of her mother and her siblings, she was going to miss them, she had no doubts about that. She remembered the tears on her mother's face, and she found herself almost sobbing. The face of her brothers came into the picture. The young boys were happily saving at her contrary to her mother. She wished she could have the innocent peace of mind that that they had.

Felix wriggled his way through the crowd looking for his bride. He had no idea what she looked like, but she hoped by chance or one way or another, he would be able to identify her. He glanced around, looking at the faces of the arrivals. He wasn't excited to meet his bride. The truth was that his mother was worried that he was getting old and yet he wasn't married. Typical Nigerian mothers. She had been screaming for over a year that she wanted grandchildren and he had only agreed to get married just to please her. The expenses of the engagement and the visa fee for his bride had eaten deep into his savings.

Marriage was the last thing on his mind until his mother coerced him into it. Raised in a polygamous home and with four siblings looking up to him, Felix's choice was to continue to take care of his mother and siblings but at her mother's insistence, he had to do her wish. Felix first came to the United States about six years earlier on a four years travel visa. After his visa had expired, he tried unsuccessfully to apply for permanent residency. For the past two years, he had been trying unsuccessfully to get permanent residence. The best he got was a renewal of his visa for another four years. He had a clean record. He had not committed any crime and he had been extremely careful of the company he kept so as not to be implicated. But all were not enough to get him the permanent residency he so much desired. After his first visa expired, he was stripped of his work permit and despite managing to renew his visa; his application for a work permit was declined on numerous occasions. In order to survive, he had to take on to driving taxis at nights while he hoped that one day, his application for work permit would be granted.

He could not risk returning to Nigeria because of the fears of having his visa cancelled; hence he had to lie to his mother that he was unable to secure the necessary paper works that would have enabled him to travel back home. He hated the idea of having a woman to fend for and take care when he was barely surviving and had so many responsibilities on his shoulders. He was jerked back to reality when he heard someone call his name.   He looked around the crowd, trying to figure out who had called his name. He was shocked to see a young girl waving at him. He wriggled his way through the crowd and went to where she stood.
'Are you Mr. Felix?' the young girl asked.
Felix nodded, hoping that for the love of Christ the young girl standing in front of him was not his bride.
'Are you Benjamin Beauty?'

'Yes sir,' Beauty replied timidly, her knees were shaky, and she feared she would collapse in no time. She was so anxious that she could bet that she would not survive this encounter. It was a truly embarrassing moment. Felix kept mute. Beauty was expecting him to say something but his silent further unnerved her. 'Mr. Felix?'

'Oh Beauty, it's good to finally meet you.' He managed to force a smile.

'You are not excited to see me. I thought you would be happy meeting me for the first time.'

Felix sighed. The girl might be young, but she was smart. He hated to admit to himself that he wasn't excited about meeting her. She was a young and beautiful girl; there was no doubt about that. She had the features of an adult; he could not deny that as well. Yet she was much younger than what he had in mind. Felix tried to blame is lack of excitement on her tender age but on a second thought, he admitted that he had never been excited about the marriage stuff and would not have been excited even if she was much older than she was. 'Ermmm, I'm so sorry about that,' he finally said after a long silence that appeared to have lasted for centuries. 'This is really embarrassing, I must admit. You're right. I'm not excited, but that's simply because you appear much younger than I imagined you are.'

'I'm not as young as you think sir; I'll be eighteen in the next six months.'

Felix was indifference. As far as he was concerned, that made little or no difference to him. 'That's alright,' he said, managing to force a smile. He could tell by the look on her face that she knew that the smile was not genuine. 'How did you manage to recognize me?' He asked, purposely diverting from the issue of her age. 'I was afraid I would never be able to find you.'

Beauty smiled, managing to put aside her timidity. 'I've seen your pictures,' she replied. 'My mother even gave me one to bring along with me and I stared at it so many times during the flight. Let me show you, it's here,' she bent to unzip one of her boxes, but Felix stopped her just in time. 'No, don't bother showing me, I believe you.'

  Beauty raised her head to look at him. She stood up slowly, feeling rejected.

Felix noticed that she felt bad with what he said. He decided to try at least pacifying her. 'Look Beauty, I didn't intend to make you feel bad. I only meant that since it's my picture then I obviously know what I look like so there's no real need for you to show me. But if you really want to show me, then you could show me at home, I'd be happy to look at it.'

'It's alright sir, I understand.' She replied.

'And listen, if we are going to get married, then there's no need for you to address me as sir. I'm your fiancé and this is not Nigeria.'

'Alright, Mr. Felix...'

Felix sighed deeply in frustration. 'And no "mister."' He said as calmly as he could, tightening his jaws to prevent himself from losing his cool.

'Alright Felix.'

'Good! I love fast learners.' He grabbed her luggage and asked her to come along with him. Beauty followed him without hesitation. He led her to his taxi and put her luggage in the trunk of the taxi. Then he asked her to sit in the front seat while he took his seat behind the wheelbase and drove off.

CHAPTER FIVE

THE first month of living with Felix was neither uneventful nor spectacular for Beauty. She was still learning to adjust to her new environment and had heartedly made friends. Felix had been kind to her. He had taken her for shopping and to other various attractive places to make her feel at home. But despite all his best efforts, she never felt at home. Something crucial was missing and Beauty was smart enough to notice it. Felix didn't love her. He was as detached from her as the South Pole was from the north. She liked him no doubt. She even thought he appeared younger than his age might suggest, and she came to realize that he was a hard-working man who would rather have permanent residency and a work permit than be married. She had to make do with what she had, always trying to please him and make him love her. Two nights before her departure for United States, her mother had sat her down and discussed with her for several hours tips and tricks that would help her easily settle down in her husband's house and navigate through the challenges that she might encounter.

She had spoken to her mother and brothers twice since she arrived in America. They were emotionally moments for her. Her mother was as usual been sober while her siblings were bustling with excitement. Matip even asked her when she would start sending them dollars. She laughed over the young boy's innocence. If there was anything, she had learnt in her few weeks in the America, it was that making money wasn't as easy as people back in Nigeria thought. When she mentioned the issue of starting a work to Felix, he had made it clear to her that he needed a work permit before she would be eligible to do any type of work. It was then she realized that things might not be easy as she thought that they would be. However, she didn't want to lose hope. She was determined to try all she could to ensure that her marriage to Felix and her stay in the United states were both successful.

Not being loved by her husband was one of her biggest fear and she felt so bad to realize that the fear had indeed manifested. Sometimes she would cry because she missed home, sometimes she cries because she wished that her husband loved her more. He took care of her no doubt, but the element of love which she desperately craved for was missing. She kept praying and hoping that things would turn around soon. She was optimistic and totally submissive to him and avoided doing anything to get on his nerves.

Much to Felix's credit, he had not takeout his frustrations on her. He was overwhelmed by her tender age and was not really prepared to shoulder her responsibility in addition to his own family's responsibilities. He tried to give her everything she wanted and did his best to make her feel at home, but he couldn't bring himself to love him. At a point in time, he thought of telling her to find her way and go for another man who was much younger and richer. But he felt it would be cruel and unwise on his path since the young lady was still settling down to her new environment. He however hoped that one day; she would realize that he didn't love her and then leave for a much younger man. He was still trying unsuccessfully to secure at least a work permit that would enable him work freely and his latest application had been knocked back.

Beauty was struggling to adapt to her new surroundings. It was the longest time ever she had been away from her mother and her siblings; it definitely took its toll on her. Sometimes, she wished that her siblings and her mother were with her. She missed them, no doubt but she had not anticipated that she would miss them as much as she did. Sometimes, she'd lock herself up when Felix was away and cry. The fact that Felix didn't love her didn't help matters. She was living with him, but in truth, she was as lonely as ever. The transition to her new environment had been nothing but easy. Things would however get better for her when she met Peace, a young Nigerian girl who stayed in the neighborhood. It all happened one afternoon when she was returning from the grocery store. As she walked home, she noticed that a lady was staring at her in the distance. When she got close to her, she politely greeted her and the lady replied warmly, complimenting her beauty thereafter.

'Thank you,' Beauty replied, with a blush. It had been long she heard a sincere compliment from someone. All she ever got were compliments from men who wanted nothing more than to get under her panties.

'Are you new here?' The lady asked, flashing her a smile that could melt the toughest of heart. She was tall and darned skin. Her hair was black and plaited into long braids. She appeared like an eighteen or nineteen-year-old damsel and Beauty thought that she must have been around in America for quite some time. She had the look of someone who was familiar with the environment.

'Yes,' she replied. 'I'm new.'

'In the states as well?'

She nodded.

'Hmm hmm. What's your name?' She asked.

'My name's Beauty.'

'Wow. As anyone ever seen such an amazing and true reflection of a name? I'd bet no name would ever fit you better.'

Beauty blushed again. 'Thank you. You must be a poet.'

The lady smiled. 'I'm not, but maybe one day I might try my hands-on poetry.'

'That's nice.'

'I'm Peace,' she extended her hand for a handshake. 'Nice meeting you Beauty.'

 'It's nice meeting you too,' she smiled.

Both ladies chatted for about ten minutes before parting ways. Peace pointed her house to her, and Beauty did the same. They exchanged phone numbers and promised to keep in touch with each other.

Beauty was excited to make her first friend. She had never really had someone to talk to and she was glad that Peace had come by at the right time. True to her words, Peace called her later in the evening. She was excited to talk to her again.   It was during their conversations that Beauty realized that she was nineteen years of age. She was in her first year in college studying Biochemistry and she had her high school education in the states as well. Unlike her, she was from an affluent family and her parent could easily afford whatever she wanted. She told her she would be going to see a movie with some friends the next day and asked if she would like to join them. Beauty wasn't sure if Felix would allow her to go, hence she told her that she would get back to her the next day. She also told her that she didn't have money to purchase the ticket, but Peace assured her that she will take care of all the expenses. They bade each other goodbye after many minutes of chatter.

When Felix arrived later in the day, Beauty excitedly told him about her new friend. Felix in his usual manner was nonchalant. He didn't care too much about her, much less who she met or how she was living her life. Beauty knew that. She wouldn't have told him about her anyway, but she thought it was necessary to enable her obtain permission to go with her to see a movie.

'Can I ask you for something?' She asked, half expecting him to turn down her request.

'What is it? I'm all ears,' he answered, avoiding her gaze.

Beauty knew as usual that he would be nonchalant about it. She was getting used to it and didn't really care now. All she cared about was to spend more time with her new friend and she happened to be the only person who was willing to listen to her. 'Peace invited me to see a movie with her tomorrow.'

'And?'

'I'm asking if I could go.'

Felix thought about it for a while. It was dangerous to thrust her into the hands of someone she had only just met but on a second thought, he thought that it might provide an avenue for her to meet other guys and probably leave him for one of them since she knew that he didn't love her. 'It's alright,' he finally said after carefully considering it. 'It's alright, you can go.'

Beauty was so excited that she forgot herself completely, jumped on him and threw her hands around him in a warm embrace. She could tell he was as shocked as she was when she regained her composure. She should not have done that, she thought as she carefully let go of him from her embrace which went without being reciprocated. She had embraced him not because she was excited that he permitted her to go, but because she would be seeing her friend again and spending some time with her. 'I'm sorry,' she apologized solemnly when she returned to her senses.

'Hmmm. It's alright. I just want you to be careful and stay safe. Don't drink, don't smoke and don't stay outside late.'

'I'll do as you've said. Thank you.'

'Good. I believe she understands this country better than you do and she will put you through adequately.'

'She will. You have nothing to worry about,' she said, trying to assure him.

'Hmm.'

Beauty couldn't wait for the next day to come. She had called her excitedly that night to inform her that she would be interested in seeing the movie with her after all. Peace was excited as well. She was happy to make a new friend from Nigeria. For the first time after arriving in America, Beauty had something to excitedly look forward to. Shortly before sunset the next day, Peace drove to her apartment to pick her up for the movie. Beauty was excited. There were two white ladies in the car and Peace introduced them to her as her course mates. Beauty was happy to meet them. As they drove off, they engaged her in a chat and asked her questions about herself and Nigeria. She was however careful not to give too much information away about herself to strangers. She couldn't trust them as much as she trusted Peace yet.

Peace bought their tickets and they went into the Cinema. The movie showing was John Wick Part III. Beauty enjoyed every bit of it. She had no doubt that Hollywood was way beyond, Nollywood, their Nigerian counterparts and wished that Nollywood could step up their game considerably. As much as she loved the movie, she loved the popcorn even more and a part of her wished that it doesn't finish when it did. After the movie, Peace's friends left while Peace took her to a restaurant. Beauty was pleased to have met them. One of them was Kathleen. A blonde with a tan skin and blue eyes, while the other one was Claire, a red head with tan skin as well but green eyes. Both were as welcoming and friendly as Peace had been to her. She admired them for having no concerns concerning her color. She had read of the prevalence of racism in America and hope that she never experienced such ugly incidents.

The restaurant Peace took her to served Nigerian dishes. Beauty was glad that she had Nigerian food to eat once again. Felix had always told her that they could always not afford to eat Nigerian foods because it was expensive. They ordered the food of their choices and Peace ordered a bottle of red wine as well. Peace told her that the restaurant was her favorite as they were the only Nigerian restaurant in the neighborhood.

'Their food is so nice that even white men come here to have a taste of it,' she told her over the course of their meal. 'The downside to it is that it is super expensive. However, I don't mind if I'm getting value for my money.

Beauty thought that corroborated Felix's claim that Nigerian food was expensive. She never doubted him; she only wished that they could afford it.

'So, tell me,' Beauty began as she poured both a cup of red wine each. 'What brought you to America?'

Beauty sighed. 'Marriage.'

'What do you mean?' Peace's eyes went wild in confusion.

'I'm engaged. I came here to be with my fiancé. Our wedding is in about six months and we'll be getting married here.'

Peace couldn't hide her astonishment. 'Engaged? You appear too young for marriage.'

'That is what my fiancé thinks as well. Since I've been with him, he has never showed me real love. And then he constantly complains of having so many responsibilities on his shoulder and how he couldn't afford to take care of a wife for now.'

'How old are you?'

'I'm seventeen. We'll be getting married after my eighteenth birthday.'

'Hmmm,' Peace sighed. 'Why did he decide to marry you when he knew that he wasn't ready to cater for a wife yet?' She was puzzled.

'Perhaps due to family pressure.'

'Oh men! Who does that in this twenty-first century?'

'Nigerians.'

'That's serious.'

'Perhaps they thought he was getting old and his mother wanted a grandchild badly.'

'How old is he?'

'Thirty-five.'

Peace almost choked on her drink. 'Are you serious?'

She nodded. 'Absolutely.'

'Oh, come on. That's eighteen whole years older than you. That's ridiculous.'

'Maybe, maybe not. I never met him until I came here. Even the engagement was done in his absence.'

'That's quite serious. Listen Beauty, if you don't want to marry him or something or you feel you are being coerced into marrying him, then we might be able to do something about it. We could get some human rights organizations to take up your case and fight for you.'

'No. I love him.'

'Sounds more like you are dependent on him.'

'He promised to send me to school. In addition, my father died some years back and things have been tough since then. I and two of my three siblings even had to drop out of school. I know my mother wants the best for me. She thinks that coming to America would increase my chances of becoming a medical doctor and lift the family out poverty. It's been really though.'

'I can't relate Beauty, but I can understand. It's though coming from a non-affluent background. However, I want you to know that you have my own hundred percent supports. If you need anything or any help do not hesitate to let me know.'

'I'm finding it different to adjust to my new environment. He's not making things any easier for me. He doesn't maltreat or abuse me, but it's just that he doesn't love me. And he doesn't even try to hide it.'

'I would consider dumping him if I were you. That's probably what he wants anyway.'

'It's not as easy as that. I'm barely one month old here, I have no house and no source of livelihood of my own and he is the only one I know in this country.'

'You know me now. You know Claire and Kathleen as well. They are really nice people.'

She smiled. She was grateful to have someone as amazing as Peace was in her life. She would easily had fallen into depression of she didn't meet Peace. She was her saving grace. 'Thank you. I really appreciate your kind gestures. It means so much to me than you could ever imagine.'

'You're welcome Beauty. We owe humanity a lot of kindness and for the world to become a better place; it has to start with us.'

'I'm with you on that,' Beauty replied. 'I am however hopeful that my marriage is going to work. I keep praying and working hard to ensure that every time turns out well. There are so many people looking up to me and I can't afford to disappoint them. With God all things are possible.'

'Hmmm. I envy your faith Beauty,' said Peace. 'And I wish you all the very best.'

'Thank you.'

CHAPTER SIX

BEAUTY and Peace became best of friends in no time. For Beauty, she was eternally grateful for her company and how she helped eased the difficulties of settling into her new environment. Although the climate had had an adverse effect on her, Peace had been on hand to help her through and give her tips on how to get along and adapt to her new surroundings. The companionship that she so much craved from her relationship with Felix was overflowing in her friendship with Peace. True to her name, she had brought peace and calmness into her and restored her hope.

For Peace, it was more about having a true Nigerian friend and someone to look out for. All her life people had been looking out for her and treating like a spoilt child. She wanted to be brave, to be on her own and live her own life. Tired of been baby-seated in Nigeria, she insisted on coming to America for her high school and college education when she was twelve. Although her choice was initially met with stiff resistance from her parents, she eventually had her way when her older siblings interfered. She was happy to have a life of her own and live independently of preying eyes and overprotective parents. And after many years of being over protected, she finally had someone to protect.

One morning, Beauty complained to Felix about feeling dizzy. She had never had that kind of feeling all her life. Sometimes, it was headache, or she had to throw up at a point in time or another. Felix knew what it meant at once. She was most likely pregnant. He asked her the last time she had her menstrual flow and she replied that she hasn't seen it since the first week she arrived in the country. She was due for another for almost a week, yet there was no sign of it. Felix decided not to jump into an early conclusion. Even though he knew that she was most likely to be pregnant, he still wanted to be medically certain.

Later in the day, they went out and brought a home pregnancy test kit for her. Felix was devastated when she tested positive. Aside the fact that there wedding was about six months away; he knew he should not be having sex with her. Their Christian faith forbade it and that was why Beauty's mother had been so insistent on her daughter staying in a convent until after their wedding. He could not even blame the young girl. He was the one who did not allow her to go stay in the convent even when she had categorically told him that her mother would not approve of them staying together before marriage. He hated to admit that a part of him wanted her company-and things had grown to the extent that they had sex.

Beauty was reluctant the first time it happened. He could still remember clearly how it had happened that first night. She had always reminded him of her mother's decision on staying at the convent until after marriage because they had to keep the bed undefiled. She never wanted to give herself to her. But Felix had been adamant. He started by touching her softly all over her body until the young lady became powerless to stop him. Then she moved on and gently caressed her. Once he placed his lips on hers, sweet sensations ran down Beauty's body. He knew she was sexually inactive. In fact, she had never been caressed or kissed before. He had to take things slowly with her.
'I can't do this,' she whispered softly into his ears.'
'There is nothing to worry about,' he tried to reassure her.
'My mother won't be pleased with me; God won't be pleased with us as well. We are supposed to keep the bed undefiled.
'And who said we are defiling the bed? Aren't we going to get married?'
Beauty could be forgiven for being swayed by the mention of marriage. She didn't want to do anything that could make him lose interest in her. She was already fighting to win him over and pushing him away was the last thing on her mind. 'Would it be painful? She asked resignedly.
'Only because it is your first time, yes. It would be a little painful.'
And that was how Felix came to deflower her. For several days after losing her virginity to him, she was moody and felt like she had committed a great sin. But she comforted herself with the fact that they were engaged and going to get married soon enough. On the other occasions that it had happened, she gave herself willingly to him since he had managed to convince him that they were going to get married anyway. To her surprise however, it didn't appear like he was starting to like her. He was only nice to her whenever he wanted to have sex with her.

He felt ashamed at the same time. They were not supposed to be having sex, he knew it. He had managed to coerce the young girl into having sex with him and there was no one to blame but himself. He thought he had no business having sex with a girl he deemed too young and was even praying she left him. He made up his mind on what to do. He was definitely not ready to become a father yet. He was finding it difficult to love and accommodate her and now that a child was in the picture. He couldn't afford to take care of the mother and the child at the same time when he was the breadwinner of his family. There was just too much responsibility on him and becoming a father would do nothing but add to his already huge burden.

Beauty's excitement about having her first child were short-lived when Felix became even more detached from her. Although she never wanted a child outside of wedlock, she had to embrace it since it was already on the way. She felt she had been forced to grow up beyond her age too quickly. With their wedding a few months away, she wondered how she would walk down the aisle with a man who was not in love with her. Her mind flashed back to the words of Prophet Elano. He had warned her not to go ahead with the wedding, but she had refused. Deciding that it was better to marry the man than to sit at home and wait for a miracle that didn't appear forthcoming. Despite the obvious setbacks she had encountered, she was determined to ensure that the randy prophet didn't have the last laugh. She became more prayerful and committed. If God was the one who turned the situations of people like Sarah and Hannah around in the bible, then she believed that God was more than capable of turning around her situation for good.

All her hopes appear to be heading down the drains when Felix took her in his taxi to a hospital. He had told her that he wanted her to register for antenatal as soon as possible and Beauty was excited at the prospect of starting her antenatal. Felix promised to be back shortly and left as soon as he dropped her off at the hospital. She met with a young male doctor and he referred her to another doctor. The doctor, a female gave her a scrutinized examination. That was when she began to suspect foul play. The doctor prescribed some drugs and told her to get them at a pharmacy. She wondered why they never gave her any tips on how to keep herself and her baby healthy, what are the do's and don'ts during pregnancy. While she sat at the reception, waiting for Felix to return, she goggled the drugs that the doctor prescribed for her on her Smartphone and realized what they were meant for. She was disappointed and angry at Felix at the same time. She wanted to cry but she managed to hold back her tears. She had been through so many challenges and she was yet to see any that crying had ever stopped. She made up her mind to be strong and bold. She was going to confront him over it. Enough of being treated without love and like an unwanted guest. If he didn't want to marry her, then he should tell him so she could plan the next phase of her life.

Felix arrived later and met her seated at the reception. He looked relieved than when he had left, and Beauty suspected he was happy to be getting rid of the pregnancy. 'How did it go?' He asked, beaming with a smile.
Beauty managed to hide her teary face. 'Not bad. I'll tell you more in the car.'
'Alright. Let me see the doctor's prescriptions.'
Beauty handed him the prescription note. He nodded as he glanced through it. 'We'll just get them at a pharmacy along the way.'
'Alright.'
He held her hand and led her to the car. Once they were inside, he started the car and drove off. 'Oh now, so tell me how it went.'
'According to your plan.' She simply replied.
'Excuse me?' He appeared to be taken aback.
'You heard me Felix. I said everything went right according to the way you planned it.'
'I don't understand. What do you mean?' The confusion written on his face appeared so innocent and Beauty was almost tempted to believe that he didn't truly understand.
'You colluded with the doctor to abort my baby. I know of everything.'
Felix pulled up by the side of the road. His face creased in complete shock. 'What are you talking about? From where you got that?'

'Don't you try to feign ignorance Felix! I'm seriously disappointed and angry with you. Look at the prescription the doctor gave me. Those are standard abortion drugs. I might be young but I'm not stupid. I know what antenatal is supposed to look like. But this, it was nothing of sort.'
'Look, Beauty I'm sorry but you have to understand...'
Beauty cut in angrily. 'Understand what? That you tried to kill my baby without my knowledge?'
'It's my baby as well...'
'That gives you no right to kill him! And without my consent for that matter. The least you could have done was to inform me that you didn't want the baby and that I should abort. But what did you do? Put my life at risk and try to kill my baby without my knowledge? That's so cruel and inhumane of you.'
'I can't take care of you and the child Beauty. I simply do not have the financial capacity yet. I have a lot of siblings back at home and the last thing on my mind right now is to become a father,' he explained.
'Yet you had the guts to sleep with me without protection when you knew the last thing on your mind was to become a father? Felix, it is now so obvious that you don't love me despite all I do to please you,' by this time she was in tears already, but she managed to fight them back. 'Another thing is that you intend to kill my baby without my knowledge and put my life at risk in the process.'
'I'm sorry Beauty. I'm sorry. Please try to understand and reason with me. I knew you were excited about having the baby and I didn't want to hurt you by asking you to abort it. Please don't be mad at me.'
'Please drive.'
'Beauty please.'
'Felix please drives. Your apologies mean nothing to me. Just drive to the pharmacy and let's get the drugs. You don't want the baby, fine. Then let's get rid of it, if that's what would make you happy.'

FELIX was visibly dejected. He was starting to regret his action. Although, he decided that she should keep the child, the deed had already been done. He knew he had so much to do to convince Beauty to trust her again. The young lady had called her mother the previous and informed her of Felix refusal to allow her to stay at the convent pending their wedding. She told her of how she had lost her virginity and became pregnant and how he attempted to abort the baby without her consent. Queen was angry. She had dashed to Ude's place and informed her of what was happening. Ude had in turn called Wemi and informed her of the happenings. All three women were displeased with the situation and Wemi assured her that she was going to have a word with her son. She apologized for her son's nasty behavior and promised that things would get better between them.

The previous night, Felix had received a call from Beauty's mother warning her sternly against aborting the baby. She told him that if he is no longer interested in marrying her daughter anymore, he should send her back to Nigeria alive instead of attempting to murder her by trying to abort her child without her consent. She had ended the call on the note that nothing must happen to her daughter otherwise, she would go to any length to make sure he paid for his misdeeds. Just when he was still reeling from the effects of the calls, his mother's call came in just in the morning. He knew it was his mother who had coerced him into getting married, but he could not blame her for his misdeeds.
'You have a family now Felix,' his mother had told him. 'Take care of your wife and your child. Your siblings and I will manage to get along. If God blesses you and you think there's something you should do for us, then please don't hesitate to do it. We are your family and we want the best for you, and we will never stop praying for you. Your efforts are acknowledged. Now it is time to pay more attention to your own family. Embrace your child and your wife. God doesn't approve of abortion.'

His mother's words had been a soothing balm. He decided to man up and accept his responsibility. Still he knew he had so much to do to fix his broken relationship with Beauty. He did all he can to make it up to her. He took her to another hospital and registered her for antenatal. A month after her eighteenth birthday, they got married in grand style. Few months later she put to bed and gave birth to a bouncing baby boy. Thereafter, he saved up some money and put her in high school. She came through with flying colors and was given a full university scholarship to study medicine. While in college, she applied for permanent residency and she was granted, her brilliance and excellent performance in the scholarship examinations paved the way for her.

Felix was granted a permanent residency as well by virtue of his wife being a permanent resident. As a permanent resident, he didn't need a work permit to work. He quit the taxi business and got a job as a clerk in an insurance company. He was glad that he decided to accept responsibility for Beauty and his child. He didn't know how it happened but now he loved Beauty more than he could ever had imagined. It was like a love made in heaven. Queen was happy that things had eventually turned out well and so was Ude and Wemi.

~~~~   ~~~~   ~~~~   ~~~~

It had been twenty-four years since they got married. Beauty and Felix now have four kids together. Beauty is now a renowned medical doctor with several doctorate degrees under her belt. She was also a national award winner and had won several accolades much to her credits. Her siblings were also grown, happily married and doing well in their respective careers. Samuel became an Engineer while Matip a Lawyer and
~~~~

Joel, the last child is an Accountant. All thanks to Beauty who ensured that they got the best quality education. Her sheer determination and perseverance saw her through all difficulties and the challenges that life threw at her. And she stood strong and ensured all her dreams were achieved. Her mother was by now, not only a clothing materials dealer, she became one of the biggest clothing materials dealers in the whole of their state. She never imagined that things would be as good as they turned out.

Felix was doing well in his insurance career. He had gone back to college and gotten a degree in insurance and now he was one of the top ranked workers in the insurance company where he worked. He had more than enough money to take care of his siblings and mother.

Every summer, Beauty's siblings visited her with their families and their mother. Beauty had already built an ultra-modern hospital and provided many other social amenities in her hometown.

It is safe to conclude that they all lived happily ever after.
This is just for your enjoyment; I hope you enjoyed reading it. Thank you tell next time.
About the author was a young lady married at a very tender age clueless about what marriage entails, never met the spouse the rest was mystery to God be all the glory.
Thank you.

www.ingramcontent.com/pod-product-compliance
Lightning Source LLC
Chambersburg PA
CBHW082015160726
47999CB00008B/2824